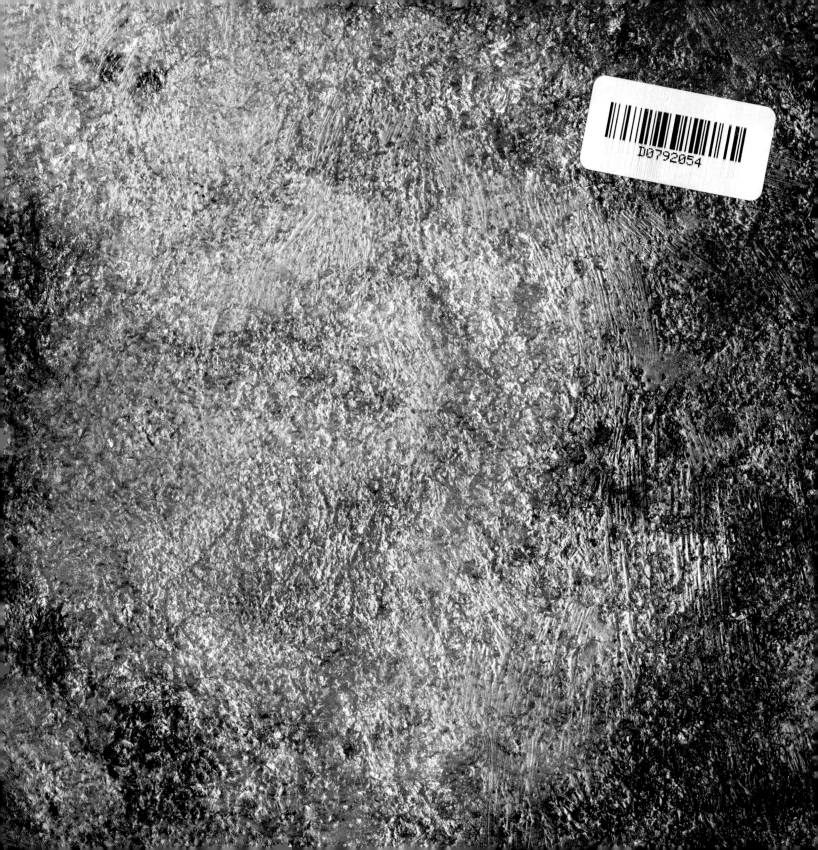

The witches and wizards of OBERIN

suza scalora

JOANNA COTLER BOOKS

An Imprint of HarperCollinsPublishers

Chamonix, FRANCE, June 14 (Euro Presse)—A team of anthropologists in the French Alps discovered a cave with signs of human habitation dating back several thousand years, according to a spokesman. To uncover the cave's entrance, the scientists triggered the collapse of a short section of the Oberin Glacier, which had kept the cave sealed for thousands of years.

According to the witnesses, the cave contained vivid wall paintings with arcane symbols and designs that dried and turned to dust moments after exposure to light. The dust was carried off in a breeze before any of the team had a chance to take samples.

While all the anthropologists in the group have solid reputations, the scientific community has largely reacted with skepticism. An American team that investigated the claim was unable to find any trace of paint, either on the wall or in the cave itself.

There are immortals, and then there are those of us who are nearly immortal, who live so long that our beginnings have faded from our memories, bleached away by ten thousand years of life on earth. I feel as though I have never been a child, as though I have been ancient since time began.

My companions, too, have been here forever with you, with the animals and plants, the rocks, the wind, the tides. We are the original magicians, the alchemists. We are the witches and wizards who collaborate with the elements, the forces of nature, to conjure, to dazzle, to bewitch.

I remember the day I realized that I was different from all the people in the valley where I lived. That night I left. I wandered the earth, searching for others like myself, slipping through villages and towns, a master of disguise. I bluffed my way through tribes of wild men. I shifted my shape into a bird and watched the world from high above. I drifted out over canyons.

In my travels I began to hear of others like myself, of witches and wizards, of sorcerers who knew how to summon the forces of nature. I heard how one, with the wink of an eye, made rock run like water. I heard of another who, with a single word, could fill a room with light, or laughter, or blinding dust. And there was one who tapped her wand and made chestnuts rain from an empty blue sky.

And I slowly met them, one by one, and together we formed our clan. We shared what we knew of the world and of our unique powers, and we continued to look for others like us.

We had homes on every continent because we crossed the world unceasingly, but it was in the great cliff palace of the Magi that we always gathered to trade stories of our journeys. We talked about the world, about its creatures, and we talked about the different spells we had developed and how to use all our various powers.

It was in the great obsidian halls of that palace where we first discussed what was to become the most important question: Were we brought together to serve some purpose? Soon, all our time and abilities were devoted to finding the answer.

The Keeper of the Moon cast decoding spells and read the stars. Another gave voice to the trees of northern forests, known for their far-reaching wisdom. And I created spirit spells that looked into the future. Slowly, a picture began to emerge, in pieces like a puzzle.

We did have a destiny, though what it was we could not clearly see. But what bewildered us more was that all signs pointed to our destiny lying in the distant future, beyond even the life span of most wizards. We were faced with our first true test: to survive across the millennia.

It would be the greatest, most dangerous spell ever attempted, and one of us would have to remain behind to cast it and, centuries later, to undo it. There was no other way.

—The Spirit Keeper

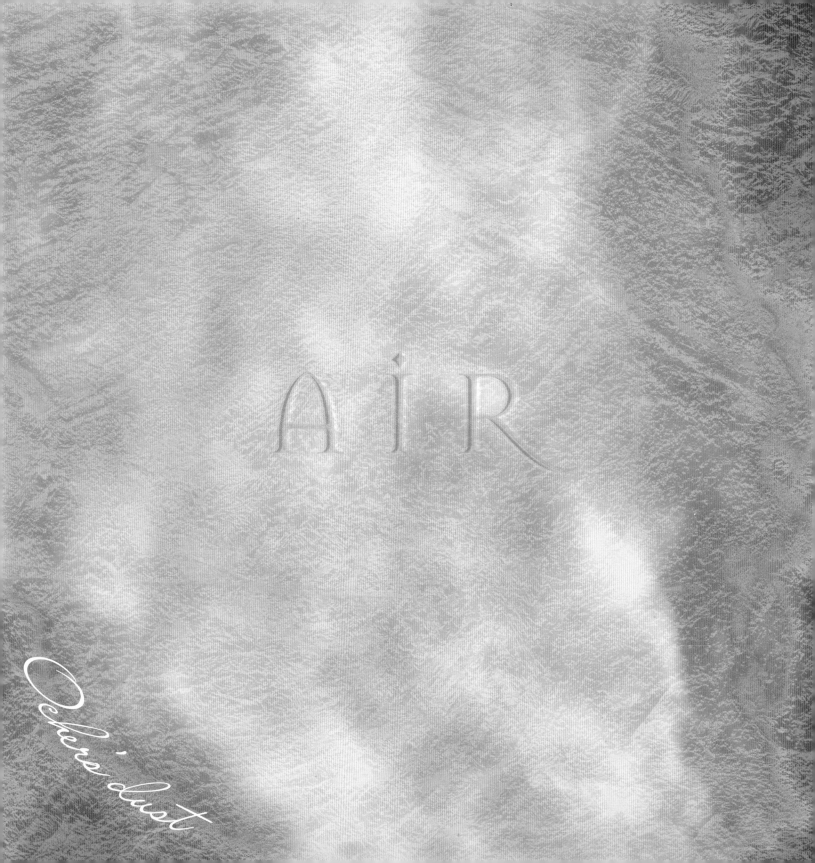

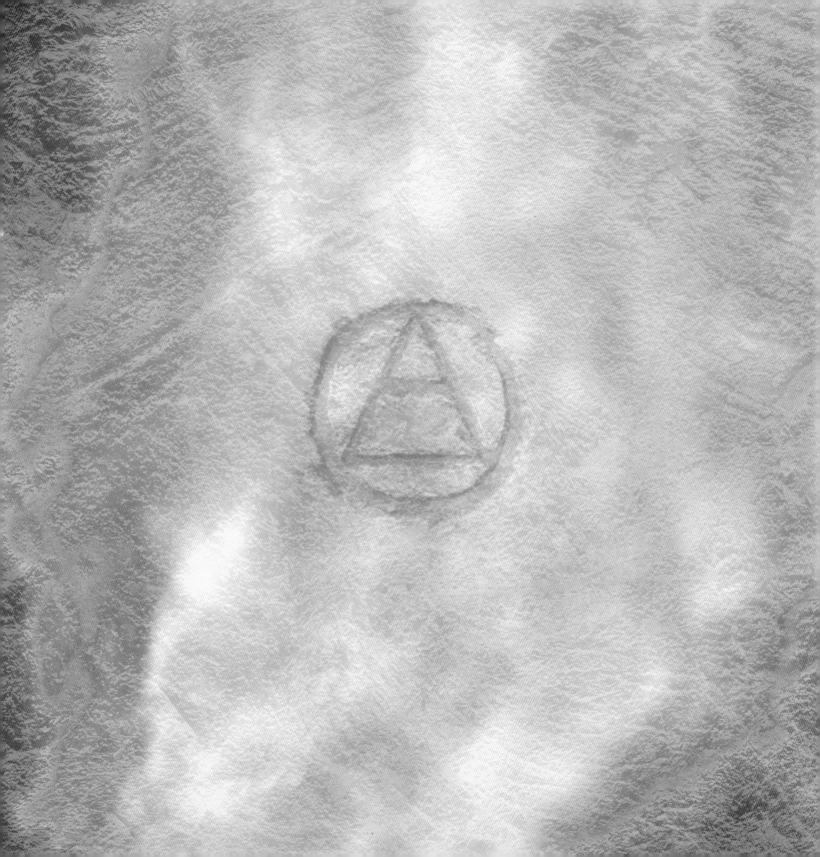

Vermilion too

Orella, Enchantress of the Dawn

O rella, strange magic.

Once, an army of giants stormed the copper city of Popol. Orella evaporated into the scent of orange blossom and drifted through the attackers, silencing them with the soft sting of childhood memories.

Sorceress Samantha Silphe

I crossed her path in the wilderness.

Because I appeared younger than she, Samantha thought she was saving me from danger. And I let her think that because she was a child alone and I didn't want to alarm her. And so we walked through the mountains, each thinking the other a helpless child, until we came to the Black River and Samantha made a bridge out of mist.

I laughed to myself, delighted.

Imagine her surprise when I turned that bridge into a carpet of stars.

and cobalt

Mazra, KEEPER OF THE WINDS She fell from the sky with a hurricane roar and followed us across the world. For centuries I feared her and the storms she conjured with her mind. Yet she watched over us, and in the end I found comfort in the rumble of her tornadoes and the high whistle of her shearing winds.

crushed

the purest

Enchantress Kedemel and Kashin, Wizard of the Woods

Kedemel and Kashin, shape shifters from the twilight forest, saw their powers intertwine with their unborn child. Their life-enhancing magic grew so strong that it overflowed and spilled into the forest around them, where the air hummed with life and flowers bloomed endlessly. When their daughter was finally born, they named her Juma, guardian of hope.

Lalezar,

WITCH OF THE FORESTS

We first encountered Lalezar

in a dark northern forest.

Wary of us, she called out, and

roots and branches sprang to life,

barring our way. Mazra raised

her arms to call a storm, but I

stopped her. Instead, I also called

to the trees, and when they

listened, so did Lalezar.

Magi
Magustus Micaboo,
The Watcher

Magi Magustus Micaboo held dominion in the silver birch
forests and soaring cliffs of the Hindu
Kush, a place where
we gathered often. Once, when his land was
invaded by the Nehood, he looked up
from his contemplation
and spoke one devastating word: SHEKAST!
Great slabs of rock tumbled down the cliffs and
turned into an army of colossal
stone soldiers. Legend
has it, they chased the Nehood all the
way to the Tangerine Sea.

for the border

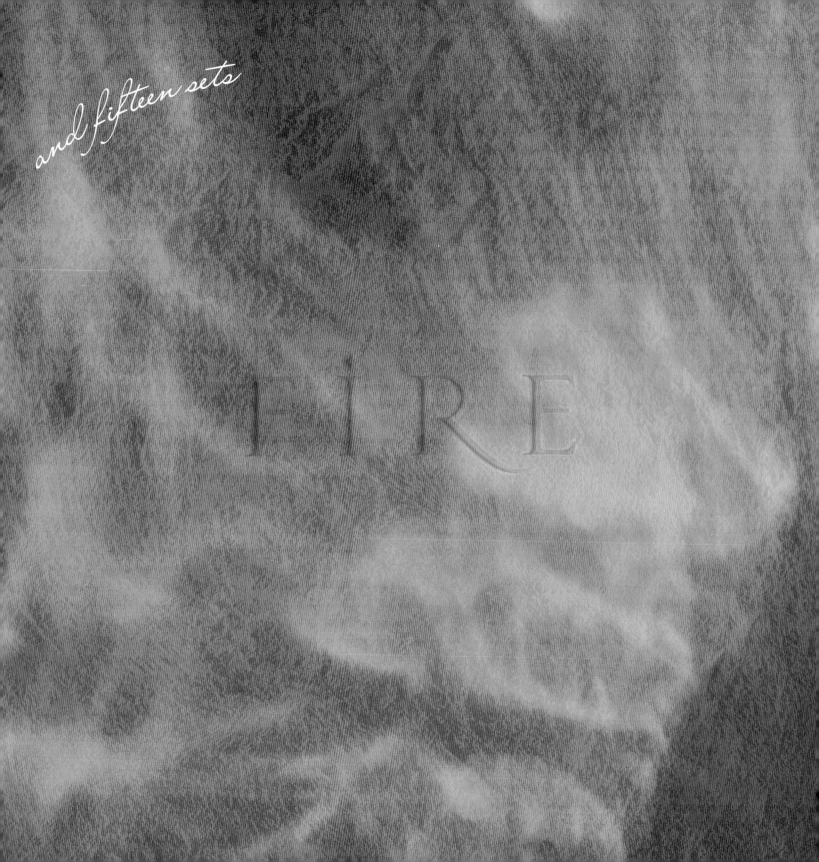

and fifteen sets

FIRE

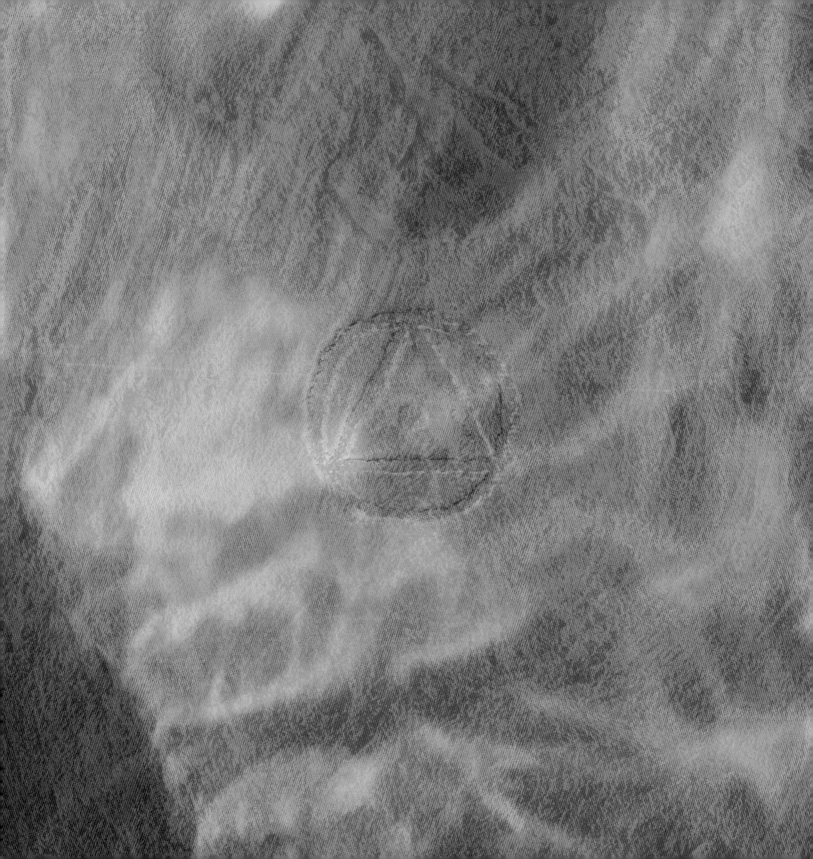

to give it order

OGMA AND MALIK, WIZARDS OF ILLUSION

Malik is a most flamboyant

wizard, a showman of sorts,

and he conjures illusions of

gigantic proportions. Once,

for no reason at all, he raised

his hands and produced a second

sun that caused a village to

wake in alarm.

OGMA

They would never have seen

night again had Ogma not

arrived and cast the opposite spell

when the real day dawned. To

this day, in the broken hills north

of the Caspian Sea, there still

exists that isolated village where

night is day and day is night.

Dami, Vermilion Bird Witch

Dami is shy and secretive, but when she weaves a spell, she comes alive. She spins, twists, and darts around, and in her wake clouds of streaming colors coalesce into mesmerizing creations.

Legends of her prowess brought me to her door, where I was greeted by a huge yellow reptile that breathed blue fire on me. It tickled. The door slammed in my face. The second time, a young girl about my size opened the door, but when I stepped toward her, she dissolved in a panic. The third time, there was a party. The house was full of all manner of people and creatures, and they invited me in. Over the course of the evening, one by one they disappeared until only Dami remained.

then brush to wall

Maruk, Warrior Wizard

Like Mazra, Maruk has always

seemed to desire nothing more

than to protect our small

clan, and he is a formidable

sentinel with power so great

that even I am left uneasy.

Once, as he dreamed, the sky

boiled above him and flashes of

crimson fire leaped from the

churning purple clouds.

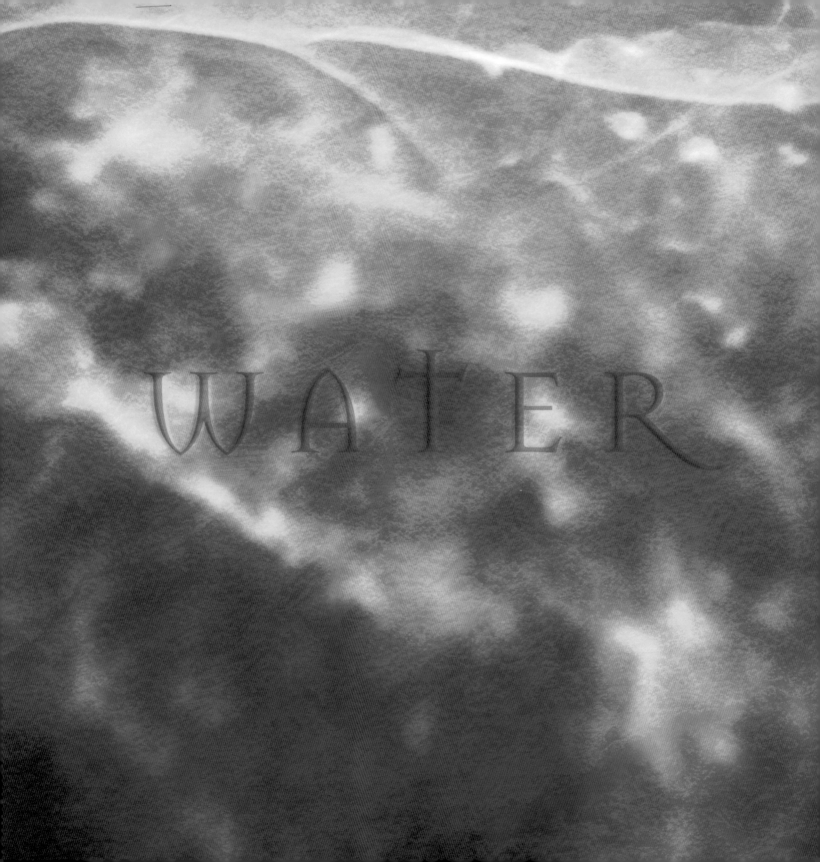

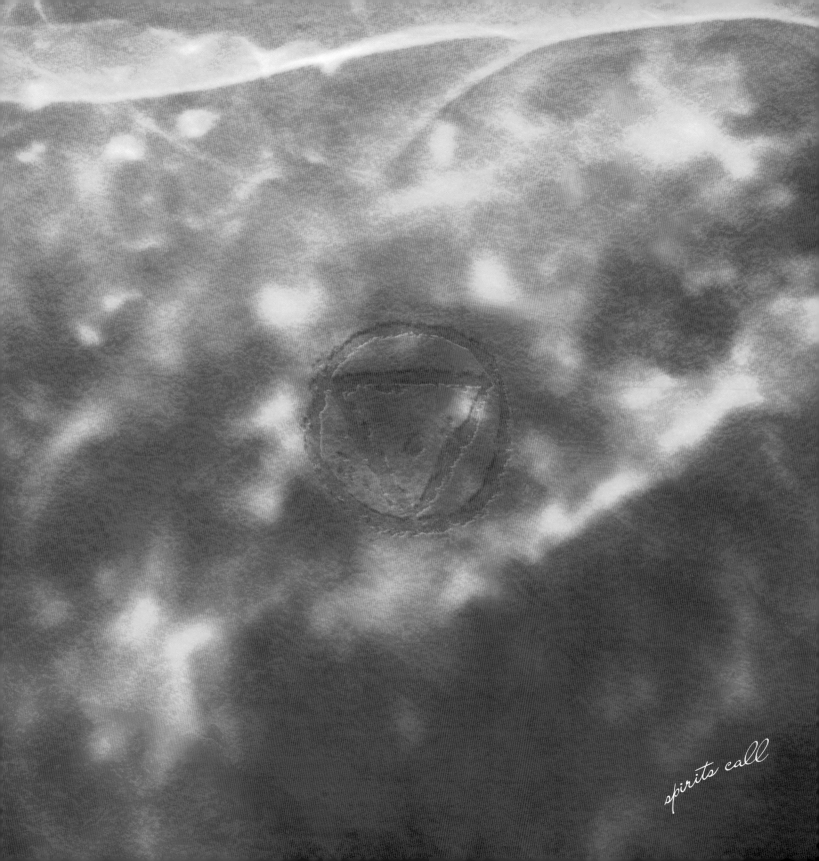

spirits call

Selendra,
Keeper of the Moon

Selendra, a sorceress of dreams and visions, was the first to join me in the formation of our group. She came to me in a dream and spoke about others like myself. Until that night, I had believed that I was utterly alone. The next day, on the shore of the Marble Sea, I met her in the flesh. That day marked the beginning of our long journey. It was Selendra who first had visions of our destiny, and when it came time to create the spell, she was the one who prepared it, though I was left behind to cast it.

Ocher's dust, vermilion too, and cobalt, crushed, the purest blue, a gram of gold leaf for the border, and fifteen vats to give it order. ...her first, then brush to wall, that would one picture of it call. For all fifteen are locked within the painted wall at Oberin.

After thousands of years,

the Keeper of the Souls appears.

He casts a light upon the wall

and utters words that free them all.

And on a wind of souls unfurled,

the wizards rise to meet the world.

Nature's forces stir and wake

as age-old spells the wizards make.

Paris, FRANCE, June 22 (BBN)—Dr. Pierre Peskit, leader of the team of anthropologists who discovered the Oberin Cave last week, has been reported missing from his home in Paris, according to local authorities. Dr. Pierre Peskit, who lectures at the European Union Institute of Sciences, is a highly regarded scholar of myth and folklore, who has written many authoritative works on ancient alchemy.

Dr. Peskit was last seen Thursday, the night a lightning storm blacked out most of Paris. That evening, neighbors claim that he was hosting a private candlelit party. The enigmatic professor, who has been a fixture in the European scientific community for as long as anyone can remember, lives alone in a small house along the river. Volunteers have posted photos of the wizened professor.

The Witches and Wizards of Oberin

Copyright © 2001 by Suza Scalora

To Carlyle, with all my love

First Edition ❖ 10 9 8 7 6 5 4 3 2 1

www.harpercollins.com

All rights reserved. Printed in Singapore.

ISBN 0-06-029535-X

Library of Congress Cataloging-in-Publication Data is available.

Story: Suza Scalora & Darius Hdim Costumes designed and handmade by m.rss. Casting: Jennifer Venditti Inc. Stylist: Elizabeth McClean Makeup: Robin Schoen & Dina Sliwiak Hair: Gerald DeCock & Stacey Ross Headpieces: Stacey Ross Props: Karen Porter & Stacey Scalora Jewelry: Manolo Collection Additional Pieces: Ligia Morris for Primal Stuff Stephanie Parc, Pippi Small, Jill Platner Book design: Alicia Mikles Production manager: Ruiko Tokunaga

Photography, art direction, set design and paintings: Suza Scalora My deepest thanks to the artists who shared their inspiration and radiant light with me.

My heart's gratitude to my editor, Joanna Cotler. Thank you for the opportunity to create my dream. Your insight, vision, and belief are invaluable treasures. Special thanks to D.J. at CYMK